Jane,

Always be un.

Katie K♥

The Unicorn With No Horn

Text copyright © 2019 by Katie Khaznehkatbi.
Illustrations copyright ©2019 by Lauren Vermeulen.
Published by Carol Khaznehkatbi, D.C.
KDP ISBN 978-1-0870-9669-8

The Unicorn
With
No Horn

To my sisters, Kourtney Rose and Kendyl Susan,

and my brother, Kyle George.

My best friends for life!

-KHK

To all the people in the world, young or old,

who don't judge others for differences.

May the future have many people like you.

-LV

In a far away land,

FAR

AWAY

LAND

YOU ARE
HERE

A unicorn was born.

This unicorn was special,
for she had no horn!

Her body was rainbow, her mane and tail pure white.

She was different,
and to her that was alright.

Her name is Rose.
She is rather pretty.

She wore colored bows
where her horn should be.

Her world was happy
from her point of view.

She hoped it would
stay that way for a long time, too.

But one day
when all was well,

Some unicorns were playing a game.
Rose tried to join in, but they started
calling her name after name.

This made her feel sad
so she ran away.
She did not understand
what the others did say.

A unicorn named Susie
saw her that day.

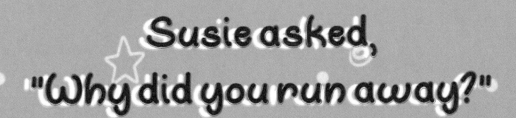

Susie asked,
"Why did you run away?"

"I'm different," said Rose.

"I'm a unique unicorn because I wear bows in place of my horn."

Susie said, "You're different, and that's okay!

It would be boring if we all looked the same way."

It doesn't matter
what others think.

It's okay to be different
and very unique.

"I'll be your friend.
You seem kind and sweet."

This made Rose happy
from her head to her feet.

Rose was glad

to have her
new found friend.

Susie helped her heart
to heal and to mend.

Rose stood tall with her bow on her head.

"You're right, Susie. Having no horn makes me special," Rose said.

ABOUT THE AUTHOR:

Katie Khaznehkatbi was born on August 4, 2010. She was 7 years old when she wrote *The Unicorn With No Horn.* She is active in Girl Scouts, enjoys playing guitar and piano, horseback riding, and is an avid reader.

She lives in Shelby Township, Michigan with her parents, little sister-Kourtney Rose, little brother-Kyle, and baby sister, Kendyl.

ABOUT THE ILLUSTRATOR:

Lauren Vermeulen has always been taught never to judge anybody for being different. She lives at her home in Michigan and will be attending College for Creative Studies (CCS) in Detroit, from 2019-2023. At the age of 18, she illustrated this book *The Unicorn with No Horn,* and made sure the main character, Rose, really came to life to help touch the lives of readers, like you! She wishes that no matter what somebody has or doesn't have, people won't treat them differently or hurt them.

68026320R00020

Made in the USA
Middletown, DE
19 September 2019